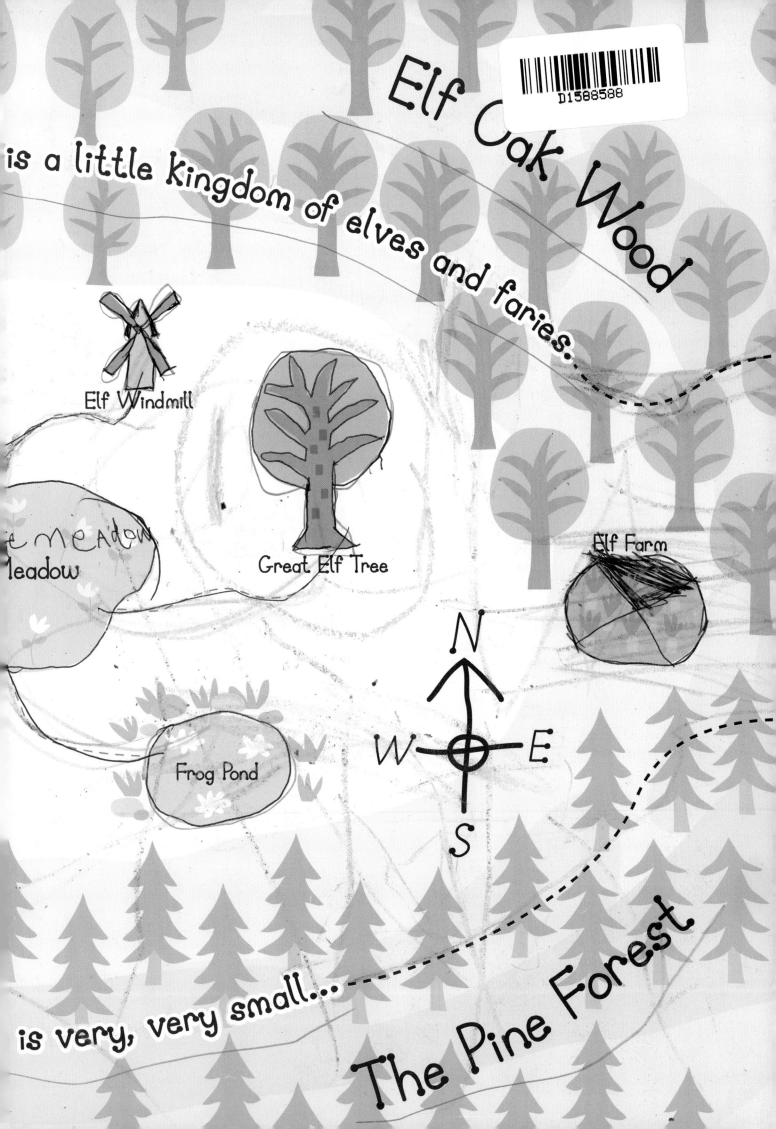

Elf Oak Wood

is a little kingdom of elves and faries...

Elf Windmill

Great Elf Tree

e Meadow

Meadow

Elf Farm

Frog Pond

N
W ⊕ E
S

is very, very small...

The Pine Forest

Contents

Ben & Holly's Little Kingdom™

This book is full of fun stuff to do! Always ask a grown-up to help before you start making things or cooking recipes.

©2011 Astley Baker Davies/Entertainment One UK Limited 2008
www.littlekingdom.co.uk

Published 2011. Pedigree Books Ltd, Beech Hill House, Walnut Gardens, Exeter, Devon EX4 4DH.
books@pedigreegroup.co.uk | www.pedigreebooks.com

£7.99

Ben & Holly's Little Kingdom™

This annual belongs to Ben, Holly and...

Kaitlyn Luara mcathar.

KAITLYN McATHAR

15 PARLEY ROAD KELTY

103 Crosscas

15 KELTY

TROVUR HOL AVINYON

road

Somewhere, hidden amongst thorny brambles,
is a little kingdom of elves and fairies.
Everyone who lives here is very, very small...

I'm Ben Elf!

And I'm Princess Holly!

Woof! Woof!

Come on, let's play!

Hello Princess Holly

I'm a young fairy princess, so I've still got lots to learn about magic! Every morning, I flutter outside to say hello to Ben Elf and Gaston the Ladybird. I live in the Little Castle with my mummy, daddy and twin sisters Daisy and Poppy.

Elf or fairy: Fairy

Height: As tall as a mouse

Best friends: Ben, Gaston and Violet

Hobbies: Casting spells and dancing

Favourite colour: Pink

Giggliest game: Hide and seek

Holly's Magic Spell Maker

Trace your finger along the spell words you like the best. Put them all together, wave your wand and say your spell out loud!

	Obbity-obbidity	Woo!
		Zee!
Zobbedy		Fizz!
	Cobwebby-ting	Ding!
Abraca...		Zoo!
	Ping Pang Pop	Poof!
Zabbedy		Whiz!
	Zibbity	Ziggle!

Now you're making magic just like me!

Princess Holly

Once, Ben and I discovered something magical about Nanny Plum! Turn to page 14 to find out what it was...

Colour me in

9

Hi Ben Elf!

Being an elf is lots of fun! Even though we don't do magic, elves are very clever. We're good at making things, climbing trees and running really, really fast. When I'm playing with my best friend Princess Holly, I give a happy toot on my elf-horn!

Elf or fairy: Elf

Height: As tall as a bird egg

Best friends: Holly, Gaston and Barnaby

Hobbies: Exploring and telling jokes

Favourite colour: Purple

Giggliest game: Tag

Let's make a space rocket

1. Paint an old kitchen towel tube in your favourite colour. Leave it to dry.

2. Find a piece of bright card, then use a pencil to trace around the lid of a jam jar. Cut the circle out and make a slit from the edge to the centre. Fold the circle into a cone and tape it onto the painted tube.

3. Cut two triangle shapes out of card. Cut a slit down the long edge of both triangles and slide them onto the bottom of the tube.

4. Find some silver foil and snip out three small circles. Glue these in a line on the side of your rocket to make windows.

Scissors are sharp! Ask a grown-up to help with cutting.

5, 4, 3, 2, 1... Blast Off!

10

Ben Elf

Colour me in ♥

One day Holly and I made cupcakes with my mum. Turn to page 26 to find out what we did while the cakes were baking in the oven...

Here Comes Gaston!

Gaston is Ben and Holly's extra special friend. Being a ladybird he has wings just like Holly's. When Ben wants to go fast he rides on Gaston's back. Gaston's cave is untidy – just how he likes it!

Animal: Ladybird

Height: As high as an acorn

Best friends: Holly and Ben

Hobbies: Barking and eating smelly food

Favourite colour: Red

Giggliest game: Fetching sticks

Race you back to the cave!

Draw a line through the meadow to show the friends which way to go. Will Gaston be the first one home?

START

FINISH

One day Ben and Holly were worried that Gaston might be sad. Turn to page 68 to see what they did to cheer him up again...

Colour me in

The Tooth Fairy

It was nearly bedtime, but Nanny Plum still had lots to do. She worked all night as a tooth fairy!

When your tooth falls out, for whom do you shout? The Tooth Fairy!

Nanny was just setting off when Holly asked...

"Can we come with you?" Nanny Plum thought for a minute. "Only if you're very quiet."

Like what?

There are lots of things we need to be careful of when we're flying at night.

SPLAT!
Ben had flown straight into a cobweb!

Nanny Plum used her magic wand to set Ben free.

"Phew!" gasped Ben.
The friends fluttered into a garden.
"What else do we have to look out for Nanny?" asked Holly.

SPLAT!

Holly had flown straight into a window!

Ben and Holly peeped through the glass.

She doesn't look very little.

What a big girl!

"Shush!" said Nanny Plum. "She's also got very big ears to hear us with!"

Nanny Plum lifted the baby tooth out from under the little girl's pillow. She had to be very careful.

That's what I call a big baby tooth.

What about the coin, Nanny?

Nanny Plum brought a shiny coin out of her travel bag.
"Oh look," she whispered. "The little girl has written us a letter."
Holly read the letter. The little girl was called Lucy.

Ben and Holly wrote a reply to Lucy's letter, and then put it under her pillow.

"Someone's coming," gasped Ben. "Hide!" Lucy's mummy walked in and pulled the window shut!

Hello! Lovely to meet you.

You're meant to be asleep.

Is that the Wise Old Elf? I need some elves to rescue us!

Lucy was very pleased with her letter. "We came in through the window," said Ben. "But now it's shut."

Lucy opened the window for her new friends. She didn't know that the elves were already on their way.

Elves to the rescue!

The Wise Old Elf was very cross when he found out that Ben and Holly didn't need to be rescued after all.

"Shush!" whispered Nanny Plum. "Can you be quiet?"
"Elves are very good at being quiet," shouted the Wise Old Elf.

And we're elves! TOOT!!!

The bedroom door clicked open. The noisy elf horns had disturbed Lucy's mummy and daddy!

Are you all right, Lucy?

It's OK, she's asleep.

The elves and fairies hid just in time. Lucy did a great job at pretending to be fast asleep.

"You can come out now," she whispered, when her mummy and daddy had gone back downstairs.

Lucy's visitors needed to head home. It wasn't long until morning!

Nanny Plum sang "When your tooth falls out, For whom do you shout? The Tooth Fairy!"

Ben and Holly giggled. Being a tooth fairy was lots of fun!

THE END!

Magical Mischief

Daisy and Poppy are Holly's baby twin sisters. They are not very good at magic yet, but they love to try out new spells! As Daisy and Poppy are so little, they are only allowed to play in the courtyard of the Little Castle.

Hop away frog, come back Nanny!

Hop away bunnies, come back elves!

Daisy and Poppy have been doing a bit of magicking today. The cheeky pair have fluttered into the meadow! The twins are using their wands to turn everyone in the Little Kingdom into animals.

Can you change everyone back again? Say the spell words and then draw a line to match the animals to the right fairies and elves.

Fly away birdie, come back elf!

Runaway kittens, come back fairies!

Make A Magic Wand

Holly would be lost without her magic wand! The fairy princess uses it to practise all kinds of new spells.

Would you like to make a special wand, just like Holly's? These pages are full of fairy magic – follow the instructions and you'll be casting spells in no time!

Glue

You will need:

PENCIL   WHITE CARD

SCISSORS   TRACING PAPER

PAPER GLUE   PURPLE FELT-TIPPED PEN

OLD NEWSPAPER   PURPLE OR SILVER GLITTER

TWO JINGLE BELLS (FROM ANY CRAFT STORE)

POSTER PAINT   STAPLER   PAINTBRUSH

A STRONG DRINKING STRAW

Ask a grown-up to do the cutting and stapling parts.

Step 1 Use a pencil to trace two star shapes onto a sheet of white card. Ask a grown-up to cut the stars out.

Use this shape for your Magic Wand star stencil

Step 2 On one of the stars, draw a smiley face. Colour the points of the star in using a bright purple felt-tipped pen, then colour the second star all over.

Step 3 Lay both of the stars on a sheet of newspaper. Dab the points of the stars with paper glue, then sprinkle pretty glitter on top. Shake the extra sparkles onto the newspaper.

Step 4

Carefully paint one side of the straw in a dark purple colour. When it has dried, turn it over and paint the other side. Leave it to dry.

Step 5 Place the first star face down on the table, then pop the end of the straw in the middle of it. Put the jingle bells in the middle too. Now carefully lay the second star on top, painted side up, trapping the bells and the straw inside.

Step 6 Ask a grown-up to staple the points of the star wand together. Give your wand a happy, jingly shake!

Now you're ready to go outside and start making magic! Look after your wand and watch out for jackdaws. Jackdaws like shiny things.

Little Castle

Tonight King Thistle is reading a bedtime story to Holly. The story is all about a place called Fairyland – how silly! The book has lots of pages, but Holly doesn't feel sleepy at all.

What do you think King Thistle's story is called? Write the title in here.

the ELf FaiRy
The FairYelf

Decorate the duvet cover on Holly's fairy bed.

Bedtime

Count the number of pictures on Holly's bedroom wall.

Colour in Holly's spinning top.

Find Holly's jack-in-the-box.

Draw a picture of the toy that Holly has left on her rug.

Point to the moon in the night sky.

Fun and Games

This is my very special cupcake recipe using flour, honey, milk, chocolate and an apple.

Ben Elf and his mum were baking in the kitchen, when Princess Holly arrived.

"Can I help?" she asked. "Fairies are good at making cakes."

Mrs Elf showed Holly and Ben how to stir the cake mixture. Holly did very good stirring, but Ben splashed cake mixture all round the bowl!

"Now we put the cake mixture in the tin," explained Mrs Elf.

Splish splash splosh sploosh!

Soon it was time to put the cakes in the oven.

"Can't we just cook them with magic?" said Holly.

"Elves don't do magic," laughed Ben and his mum. "And we're elves!"

Why don't you go outside and play for a bit?

Ben and Holly did not want to go and play outside.

"I suppose we might as well try playing a game," suggested Holly.

I wish those cakes didn't take so long to bake.

Me too!

Fun and Games

"How about tag?" said Ben "I like tag."

But you must play fair. No magic!

Ben tapped Holly on the nose. Now she was 'it'!

"Can't catch me!" he shouted. "It's not fair!" puffed Holly.

"Fairies can't run as fast as elves!" When it was Ben's turn to be 'it' Holly flew into the air.

That's cheating. We said no magic!

I'm just flapping my fairy wings.

Holly fluttered back down to the ground. Maybe it was time for a new game.

Ben and Holly decided to play hide and seek.
"But no flying!" said Ben.

"Not there..."

One... two... three... four, five, six, seven, eight, nine, ten!

Holly lifted up leaves and poked round brambles. Ben was a good hider!
"Ben!" she shouted. "Give me a clue. Please?"
Suddenly Ben's voice called out from a tall flower. "You're getting warmer!"

Holly climbed up the flower's big green stalk.
"Found you!" she giggled.

Oh! There's no one there!

"Where is he?" sighed Holly.

Suddenly Ben popped his head out from under a leaf.
"Elves always hide well," he cried.

"And I am an elf!"
Next it was Holly's turn to hide.

Ben closed his eyes and started to count.
"Ben said no flying," whispered Holly.

"But he didn't say no magic."
She looked at her wand. A teeny bit of magic would be all right, wouldn't it?

Ben found it very, very hard to find Holly. But after a while, her magic started to wear off.

"Holly's hidden too well," fibbed Ben.

The fairy burst into giggles!
"Found you!" shouted Ben.
"Oops!" laughed Holly. "I was just using a teeny bit of magic!"

Back at the Elf Tree, Holly watched Ben pop a cake into his mouth. Munch, munch, munch!

The cake disappeared. Maybe elves could do magic after all!

THE END!

Yummy in your Tummy

Ben loves baking with his mummy. When they're cooking in the kitchen, he can't resist splishing and sploshing the mixture with his wooden spoon!

Ask a grown-up to help you make a batch of Mrs Elf's scrummy elf cupcakes. This recipe will make enough for all of your friends.

Ingredients for 12 elf cakes

- 250g self raising flour
- 115g brown sugar
- 1 teaspoon bicarbonate of soda
- A pinch of salt
- 2 eggs
- 75g soft margarine
- 125ml milk
- 1 teaspoon vanilla extract
- 2 large apples
- 1 tablespoon runny honey
- 100g chocolate chips

Before you start, put on your apron and wash your hands! Always make sure a grown-up is there to use the oven and help with any tricky jobs.

1. Ask a grown-up to heat the oven up to 190°C/375°F/Gas Mark 5, while you lay 12 cupcake cases onto a baking tray.

2. Tip the flour, brown sugar, bicarbonate of soda and salt into a big mixing bowl, then give it a good stir.

3. Find another bowl, then crack the eggs open and drop them in. Now mix in the margarine, milk, and vanilla.

4. Carefully peel and grate the apples, then tip them into the egg mixture too. Stir in the honey.

5. When your egg mixture looks thick and sticky, scrape it into the big bowl of flour. Add the chocolate chips, then use a wooden spoon to stir everything together – Splish splash splosh sploosh!

6. Spoon the cake mixture into the paper cases, dolloping the same amount into each one.

7. Ask your grown-up helper to bake the cakes in the oven for 20 minutes. When they're ready, the elf cakes should be golden brown on top. Yummy!

Smoothies to Slurp

Cooking is thirsty work! Ben and his friends like to sip on smoothies made from the delicious fruit that grows in the Little Kingdom.

Ask your mummy or daddy to put two bananas in a blender with a glass of milk and a small carton of plain yoghurt. Now tip in three handfuls of fruit and whiz everything up super-fast. Tip the smoothie mixture into glasses and get slurping!

Why not try...
• Strawberries
• Blueberries
• Peaches
• Raspberries
... or a mixture of them all?

The Great Elf Hunt

Today is the Great Elf Hunt and some of the Elves are hiding amongst the branches and leaves of the Great Elf Tree. Look closely and see how many you can find!

These Elves are hiding. Tick each one when you find them!

Ben Elf

Lizzy Elf

Mrs Elf

Mr Elf

Jake Elf

Barnaby Elf

Toby Elf

The Wise Old Elf

The birds have come to see what is going on at the Great Elf Tree. Write down how many birds you see in the picture.

4

Colour in this new tree that has grown. Don't forget to add lots of leaves and fruit!

A Busy Day at Elf School

Flying and magic is not allowed at Elf School. The elves learn to build, draw and paint all by themselves!

The Wise Old Elf needs some new pictures for the classroom wall. Can you draw some for him?

Elf School is at the top of the Great Elf Tree. At Elf School, the Wise Old Elf teaches the children how to make toys.

Would you like to make a special elf bookmark to put in your favourite reading book? It's as easy as A, B, C!

1. Use a sheet of tracing paper to transfer the shape of this wobbly bookmark onto a white sheet of card.

2. Ask a grown-up to help you cut the bookmark out, then create an elf themed pattern onto both sides. Use your brightest crayons to colour it in.

USEFUL TIP! To make your bookmark extra-strong, ask your helper to cover it with sticky back plastic.

Make an

Elf Bookmark

Why not make a hole in the bottom of your bookmark, then thread through some wool to make a tassel?

Someone has come along to Elf School today who shouldn't really be there! Can you spot who it might be? Write their name below.

__ __ __ __ __

Let's play with
Ben & Holly

Would you like to play in the Little Kingdom with Ben and Holly? This game is for two players. Ask your best friend, a grown-up or your little brother or sister to play it with you. All you need is a dice and two counters or pennies.

START

1 Jump up and down three times.

2

3 Forget to put on your hat. Miss a turn.

4

9

8 Run around the room really fast.

7

6 Get a ride on Gaston's back. Go forward 3 spaces.

5

10

11

12

13 The Wise Old Elf gives you top marks in Elf School. Move to number 16.

14

19

18 You're the winner at hide and seek! Throw the dice again.

17 Pretend to toot your elf-horn as loud as you can!

16

15 Holly turns you into a frog. Go back to number 10.

20 Go to help Mr Elf deliver eggs to the Little Castle. Move back 2 spaces.

21

22

23 Pretend to ride a space rocket to the Moon. 5, 4, 3, 2, 1... blast off!

FINISH

HOW TO PLAY:

Choose one player to be an elf like Ben and the other to be a fairy like Holly. Elves should put their counters on the purple board and fairies should put their counters on the pink ones. Take turns to throw the dice and then move forward along the boards as fast as you can. Follow the instructions on each square to find out who will make it to the end first!

If you land on an elf-horn or a fairy wand follow the instructions. When you've finished take an extra throw of the dice!

START

1

2

3 Go night flying with Nanny Plum. Move to number 6

4

Stay in to read fairy stories. Miss a turn.

Tell a joke, then make a sweet fairy giggle.

7

6

Make up your own fairy spell.

10

11

King and Queen Thistle help you make magic. Move forward to 15.

Tiptoe round the room, just like a fairy.

14

19

Help Nanny Plum look after Daisy and Poppy. Go back 3 spaces.

17

Beat Ben at a game of tag! Throw again.

15

20

Stand like a statue for 30 seconds.

Your wand gets broken! Miss a turn until it gets fixed.

23

FINISH

39

Abraca-Zobbedy Zee!

Uh-oh! Holly's magic has gone wrong again! What has she turned Ben into this time? Join up the dots, then colour the poor elf in.

CROAK!

Now put a tick next to the animal's name.

Blackbird ☐ Frog ☑ Sheep ☐

Ben & Holly's Little Kingdom™

BEDTIME reading

Ben & Holly Go to the North Pole

This adventure starts at the Great Elf Tree on Christmas Eve...

Holly and her fairy friends pulled on woolly hats, then fluttered over to say hello to Ben and the elves.

"Hi Ben!" said Holly. "What's happening?"

"My dad has an important job to do," replied Ben.

Mr Elf gave a thumbs-up from the cockpit of the Elf Plane.

"Flight 1,000," he nodded. "Ready for take-off!"

Wise Old Elf explained that Ben's dad was making the final delivery of toys to Father Christmas.

"Elves work all year making toys," grinned Ben.

"Does your dad land at the North Pole?" asked Holly.

"No," said Wise Old Elf. "The toys are dropped by parachute." Once Father Christmas had got the toys, it was his job to wrap them up and deliver them to the children of the world.

"I love Christmas!" smiled Holly.
"And I love snow!"
Jake Elf nodded. "I wish it was
snowing now."
Wise Old Elf wheeled out his Elf
Weather Detector.
   "I listen to the weather through this
giant ear trumpet," he explained.
   "It's so sensitive, I can hear a butterfly
flapping its wings in Africa!"
Strawberry peered into the trumpet.
   "Can you hear any butterflies now?"
she cried.
"Aargh!" spluttered Wise Old Elf, before
announcing that it might snow... or it
might not.
Holly decided to ask Nanny Plum if it
   was going to snow. She could tell
      the future!

When Holly and her friends arrived at Little Castle, Nanny Plum was sweeping the floor in the kitchen.

"Can you tell if it's going to snow today?" asked Jake Elf.

"Yes!" replied Nanny Plum. "I'll use my special forecasting globe. It's never been wrong."

Nanny Plum gave the globe a good shake, then put it on the kitchen table. A swoosh of snowflakes started to swirl around inside the little glass dome. The elves and fairies cheered – it was going to snow today!

"Stop, stop, stop!" shouted the Wise Old Elf. "That thing can't tell exactly when it's going to snow." Nanny Plum knew it could, but just to be on the safe side she gave her magic wand a wave.

"Abracadabra, make it snow!"

"Hooray!" cheered Holly. "Nanny Plum's made it snow!"
Barnaby Elf clapped his hands.
   "Let's go and see it."
   The fairies and elves rushed up the castle stairs two at a time. But when they got to the roof, the sun was still shining. Nanny Plum's magic hadn't worked after all.

"Nanny Plum!" bellowed a voice from downstairs.
   "That's King Thistle," gulped Ben. "It must be snowing inside!"

The friends dashed into the sitting room. King Thistle was trying to read the paper in the middle of a snow shower! He looked very cross.
   "Nanny Plum," he boomed. "I'm taking away your wand until you learn how to control your spells better. Everyone out!"

Nanny Plum led the way back to the Great Elf Tree. Everyone was very disappointed not to have any snow for Christmas.

"I can hear something," said Holly.

"It's the Elf Plane!" cried Ben. "Dad's back from the North Pole!"

Ben's dad waved hello, then climbed out of the Elf Plane. Even though he'd delivered all the Christmas presents, he only had time for a quick tea break. He still had to get ready for the Elf And Fairy Feast that took place every Christmas Eve!

"Elves like working hard," he smiled. "And I'm an elf!"

Ring! Ring!

The Wise Old Elf clicked on his mobile phone.

"Mr Christmas!" he gasped. "You're missing a box of toys? Never fear, we'll deliver it at once!"

The Wise Old Elf explained that Father Christmas was missing box 571. If he didn't have those by toys tonight, some children wouldn't get their Christmas presents!

"Is it this box?" asked Ben, pointing to a big brown crate with 571 printed on the side.

Mr Elf nodded. "To the Elf Plane! Immediately!"

"Can we come Dad?" begged Ben. "Pllleeeaasse!"

As it was an emergency situation, Mr Elf decided that the fairies and elves were allowed to come. The plane got ready for take off.

"Look!" said Holly. "It's snowing."

Nanny Plum winked at the Wise Old Elf.

"You see?" she chuckled. "My snow globe is never wrong."
Ben peeped out of the window.

"North Pole here we come!"

47

It took a long time to get to the North Pole.

"Will we meet Father Christmas?" asked Holly.

The Wise Old Elf shook his head.

"Remember we never land at the North Pole. We drop the toys by parachute."

"Does Father Christmas catch them?" wondered Strawberry.

"No," replied the Wise Old Elf. "The toys are collected by Arctic elves."

After the Elf Plane had dropped off box 571, it was time to head for home.

Clunk-clank-ting!

"That sounds odd," said Nanny Plum.

Cogs and screws rattled around the engine – the Elf Plane was broken!

Everyone held on tight so Mr Elf could make a bumpy landing. It was nearly time for Christmas, but they were stuck in the North Pole!

Holly was very excited.

"Now we might meet Father Christmas!" Nanny Plum gazed into the snow. She wanted to meet some penguins.

"Penguins live in the South Pole," said the Wise Old Elf. "This is the North Pole."

Suddenly the Arctic elves arrived. The Wise Old Elf waved at one with a long white beard.

"That's my twin brother!" he smiled. The Arctic elf with the beard was three minutes older than the Wise Old Elf. When he heard that his brother was stranded, the Wiser Older Elf decided to take the visitors back to Father Christmas's house.

On the way, Nanny Plum borrowed Violet's wand. She couldn't resist casting a spell to magic up a penguin.

Luckily Father Christmas only lived round the corner.

"Here we are!" cried the Wiser Older Elf. "I built the house myself."

Holly and Ben gasped. Father Christmas's house looked just like a Christmas pudding! Even Nanny Plum's penguin couldn't help being impressed.

When they got inside, the Wiser Older Elf showed everyone around.

"I suppose it's OK," shrugged the Wise Old Elf. He didn't like not being the wisest elf anymore. Nanny Plum pointed at box 571.

"Shouldn't we be wrapping the presents now? It's Christmas Eve!"

"You're right!" cried the Wiser Older Elf. "To the present-wrapping machines!"

A line of Arctic elves were sitting at the present-wrapping machines, ready to get to work.

"Arctic elves love wrapping presents!" they cheered. "And we're elves! Toooot!"
The Wiser Older Elf was very impressed with the toys in box 571. There were robots, dolls, space rockets and cars.

"You've done a good job, brother," he said.

The Wise Old Elf beamed. "Thank you!"

"Ho ho ho!" chuckled a very loud voice – Father Christmas had arrived! He carefully picked up Ben and Holly and set them on his palm.

"I've got some work to do tonight," he smiled. "Would you like me to drop you all home? It's on my way."

"Yes please!" cried Ben and Holly.

When they got to Lucy's house, the chimney looked very small.

"We can deliver the presents for you," suggested Holly.

Father Christmas smiled. "All right!" Holly and her friends hurried down the chimney. They were just tiptoeing across the rug when Lucy's dad opened the front room door.

"That's odd," he gasped. "Some of the decorations have fallen off the tree."

Lucy's dad carefully picked the elves and fairies up and popped them on the Christmas tree.

Father Christmas piled the toys onto his sleigh, then tucked the elves and fairies into his hat. He even found a space for Nanny Plum's penguin!

"Ho ho ho," he laughed. "Off we go!"

"Have you got a present for our friend Lucy?" asked Ben. Father Christmas nodded. He had presents for all the boys and girls.

As soon as Lucy's dad had gone, Holly fluttered down from the top of the tree.

"That was close!" she gasped. The elves and fairies climbed up the stairs, then crept into Lucy's bedroom. They had enough presents to fill Lucy's stocking right to the very top!

"Ben! Holly!" Lucy had woken up!

"You're supposed to be asleep," whispered Holly.

Lucy giggled. She was much too excited about Christmas to go to sleep.

"We better go," grinned Ben. "Santa's waiting on your roof!"

The elves and fairies said goodbye to Lucy, then rushed back up the chimney. Now they were ready for Father Christmas to drop them off at the Elf And Fairy Feast!

The End

Hurray for Snow!

This morning, the Little Kingdom has turned into a winter wonderland. Ben and Holly can't wait to go outside and explore – elves and fairies love snow! Before they are allowed out, the friends have to put on their coats and hats. Where shall Ben and Holly go first? There are three paths they can take... trace the paths and find where each leads!

A

B

C

The Little Castle

The Great Elf Tree

Funny Business

King and Queen Thistle have called the fairy princesses into the throne room. They are going away for the day, so Holly will be in charge. It's a very important job – the King doesn't want any funny business and he certainly doesn't want to come back to find the kingdom covered in frogs or jelly!

Nanny Plum's Lesson

Nanny Plum is Holly, Daisy and Poppy's fairy maid and teacher. Being a grown-up fairy, Nanny is very good at flying and magic. But sometimes Nanny Plum's spells go a bit wrong. King Thistle and the Wise Old Elf get very grumpy when this happens.

Nanny Plum says that every fairy needs to follow **three** special rules. Do you know what they are? Read Nanny Plum's list, then place a big tick next to the right fairy rules. Put a big cross next to all the rules that have nothing to do with fairies at all.

1. Fairies must always look nice.

2. Fairies must run really fast.

3. Fairies must never, ever be without their wands.

4. When it's windy, fairies should be careful of flying.

5. Fairies must learn to make toys and games.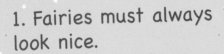

6. Fairies must wear a hat with a leaf in it.

As well as teaching little fairies, Nanny Plum does lots of housework. Today she's pegging out the washing. Use the numbers to help you pick the right crayons or pencils to colour in the picture.

BIG and small

The Wise Old Elf and Nanny Plum are taking the children on a tour of the Big Farm.

They must be careful – on the farm there are big people with very big feet!

QUESTION 1

Everyone in the Little Kingdom is very, very small. Next to Ben and Holly, the animals seem huge! Point to the smallest animals that you can see.

Chickens

QUESTION 2

Who is smaller – Rex the dog or Bessie the cow?

ELF 3

60

QUESTION 3

Which middle-sized animals have bodies covered in wool?

Sheep

QUESTION 4

Which animal is even bigger than Lucy?

cow

Colour in a tractor for every question you get right.

Meadow Maze

START

The Wise Old Elf is calling Ben and his friends to the Elf Windmill. He needs the elves to help him make some flour. Elves are always very busy indeed!

Can you help Ben and the elves find their way through the meadow? Put your finger at the start and then trace a path through the maze avoiding the leaves.

Hurry, hurry! There is lots of work to do!

TOOT!! TOOT!!

Little Looking Game

Princess Holly's bedroom is at the top of the Little Castle. If she stands on tiptoes and looks out the window, she can gaze right across the Little Kingdom.

Can you see who Holly has spotted now? You'll need to look carefully – the Little Castle is very, very tiny.

Look even closer at these pictures. Only one matches the top picture exactly. Can you see which one it is? Draw a circle around the picture that is a perfect match.

A

B

C

D

Tot up the toys

The Wise Old Elf is wise, old and an elf. As well as being a teacher, he runs the Elf Factory deep down in the roots of the Great Elf Tree. The Wise Old Elf does not like magic of any kind. He prefers to get things done with hard work.

Trace over a number for every toy that you see!

1 2 3 4 5 6 7

The busy elves in the Elf Factory have made another batch of toys. It's the Wise Old Elf's job to count them all up. How many are there?

Draw a picture of your favourite toy here.

Gaston The Ladybird

KNOCK! KNOCK!

Ben and Holly were waiting outside Gaston's cave.

"Are you coming out to play?" they asked.

Come on, let's fly!

Ben jumped on Gaston's back.

"Giddy-up, giddy-up!"
The ladybird flapped his wings. He loved playing!

As soon as they got to the meadow, Ben found a stick to throw.

"Gaston!" he called. "Fetch!"
The ladybird ran after the stick and brought it back.

Woof! Woof!

Well done!

"Clever Gaston!" said Holly.

Gaston was ready for another game.
"Do you want to wiggle your legs?" asked Holly.
Gaston rolled on his back and started wiggling.

"Holly!"
Nanny Plum rang the bell for bedtime.
"I've got to go home," sighed Holly.

"Ben! Bedtime!"
Now Mrs Elf was tooting her elf horn.
"Bye Holly," said Ben. "Bye Gaston."

The meadow started to get dark. Gaston flew
back to his cave and settled down to sleep.

When Ben and Holly arrived at Gaston's cave the next morning, the ladybird had already gone out to play.
   "Where is he?" asked Ben.

"I'm going to fetch Nanny Plum," replied Holly. "She knows all about ladybirds."

Look at the state of this cave!

"Gaston has gone," said Holly.
   Ben gulped. "Maybe we've upset him!"
   "No one could be happy in this messy, smelly cave," decided Nanny Plum.

Urgh! We need to clean up before the ladybird returns!